Franklin's Valentines

To good friends, Tarah and Caitlin Blum — S.J.
To Papa Wilf, with love — B.C.

Franklin

Franklin is a trademark of Kids Can Press Ltd.

Text © 1998 Contextx Inc.
Illustrations © 1998 Brenda Clark Illustrator Inc.

Story written by Sharon Jennings.
Interior illustrations prepared with the assistance of Shelley Southern.

Kids Can Press acknowledges the financial support of the Ontario Arts Council; the Canada Council for the Arts and the Government of Canada, through the CBF, for our publishing activity.

Published in Canada by
Kids Can Press Ltd.
25 Dockside Drive
Toronto, ON M5A 0B5

Published in the U.S. by
Kids Can Press Ltd.
2250 Military Road
Tonawanda, NY 14150

www.kidscanpress.com

The hardcover edition of this book is smyth sewn casebound.
The paperback edition of this book is limp sewn with a drawn-on cover.
Manufactured in Buji, Shenzhen, China, in 3/2013 by WKT Company

CM 98 0 9 8 7 6 5 4 3
CDN PA 98 0 9 8 7 6 5 4 3 2
CMC PA 13 0 9 8 7 6 5 4 3 2 1

Library and Archives Canada Cataloguing in Publication

Jennings, Sharon
    Franklin's valentines / story based on the characters created by Paulette Bourgeois and Brenda Clark ; illustrated by Brenda Clark ; [written by Sharon Jennings].

(A classic Franklin story)
ISBN 978-1-77138-006-5

    1. Franklin (Fictitious character : Bourgeois) — Juvenile fiction.
I. Bourgeois, Paulette II. Clark, Brenda III. Title. IV. Series: Classic Franklin story

PS8553.O85477F895 2013   jC813'.54   C2012-907880-8

Kids Can Press is a *Corus*™ Entertainment company

Franklin's Valentines

Story based on characters created by Paulette Bourgeois and Brenda Clark
Illustrated by Brenda Clark

Kids Can Press

FRANKLIN could count to ten and back again. He knew the days of the week, the months of the year and the holidays in every season. Today was Valentine's Day, and Franklin was counting the valentines he'd made for his friends. He wanted to be sure he hadn't forgotten anyone.

"Hurry up, Franklin," said his mother. "You'll miss the school bus!"

Franklin rushed to find his hat and mittens and boots. He tossed his valentines into his bag.

"I'm going!" called Franklin, and he hurried out the door.

At school, Mr. Owl gave the class a valentine spelling bee and valentine arithmetic problems. But everyone was too excited about the Valentine's Day party to think about work.

Franklin whispered to Bear, "I can't believe we have to wait until after lunch to give out our cards."

"I can't believe we have to wait until after lunch for the goodies," Bear whispered back.

At last, it was time for the party.

"You may get your valentines now," said Mr. Owl.

Franklin grabbed his bag and reached inside. He pulled out his hat, and he pulled out his mittens. He pulled out a ball and a scrunched-up piece of homework. Then he held his bag upside down and shook it.

"What's wrong?" asked Bear.

"My valentines! They're gone!" cried Franklin.

After Franklin looked everywhere, Mr. Owl let him phone home. Franklin waited and waited while his mother searched.

"I'm so sorry, Franklin," she finally said. "I found your valentines outside in a puddle of slush. The cards are ruined."

Franklin blinked away tears. He gave the phone to Mr. Owl and ran out of the room.

Mr. Owl found Franklin in the cloakroom.

"There you are, Franklin," he said. "Your friends are waiting. We can't start the party without you."

"I don't belong at the party," replied Franklin. "I don't have any valentines to give."

"I know," said Mr. Owl. "Your mother told me what happened. And I told the class."

Franklin moaned. "I guess no one's going to give me a valentine now."

"Hmmm," said Mr. Owl. "If Bear lost his valentines, would you decide not to give him a card?"

"I'd never do that!" exclaimed Franklin. "Bear is my friend."

"Maybe Bear feels the same way about you," replied Mr. Owl.

Franklin thought about that.

"Maybe," he said. He cheered up a little.

Franklin and Mr. Owl went back to the classroom.

Franklin watched as his friends delivered their cards.

As the pile of valentines in front of him grew bigger and bigger, Franklin felt sadder and sadder. There were so many, and he had none to give in return.

He sighed as he opened Bear's card.

"What's wrong, Franklin?" asked Bear. "Don't you like my card?"

"I do! But I feel bad because I don't have one for you," said Franklin.

"Oh, that's all right," said Bear. "I don't need a valentine to know you're my friend."

Franklin smiled.

Everyone gathered around as Franklin opened his other cards.

"Mine's a turtle cut-out," said Snail.

"Mine's a turtle poem," said Goose.

"And I made up a turtle riddle," said Fox.

"These are great!" exclaimed Franklin. "I just wish I had my valentines for all of you!"

"I just wish we could start eating all these goodies," replied Bear.

Everybody laughed.

That night, Franklin told his parents about
the party.

"It sounds as if you have some very good
friends," said Franklin's father.

"I sure do!" agreed Franklin. "Next year, I'm
going to make them extra-special valentines!"

"Well, you've got a whole year to get ready,"
replied his mother.

"I don't know if I can wait a whole year,"
said Franklin.

The next morning, Franklin's mother found him at his table, writing and drawing and cutting and folding.

"What are you making?" she asked.

"It's a surprise," Franklin answered.

His mother smiled. "Well, hurry up. You'll miss the bus."

But Franklin didn't hurry. He wrapped his artwork carefully and placed the package in his bag. He made sure that all the buckles were done up tight. Then he hugged the bag to his chest and went out the door.

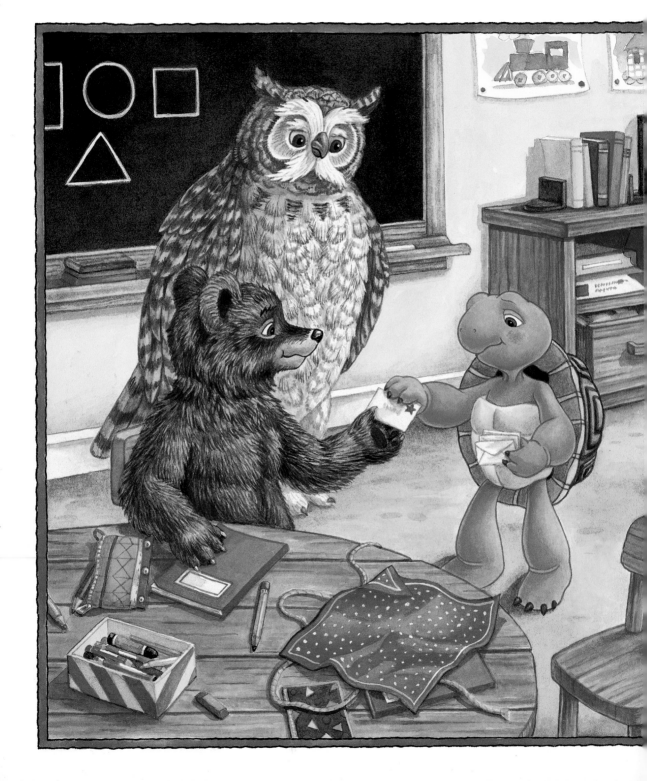

As soon as Franklin got to school, he opened his package and gave everyone a card.

"What are you doing, Franklin?" asked Beaver. "Valentine's Day was yesterday."

"Oh, these cards aren't for Valentine's Day,"
replied Franklin. "They're for Friendship Day. And
Friendship Day can be any day you want it to be."